LOVE'S PERFECT IMPERFECTION

EMMA CARTWRIGHT

CHAPTER 1

*N*aomi Hershberger was the first to rise from the pews as the ministers and Bishop Troyer stepped away from the podium. Services had only just concluded for the day and Naomi already found herself surrounded by half a dozen friends from the district, each vying for her attention.

This was commonplace for any event or gathering. The young people of the community were eager to curry favor with the lovely woman and worship days were no exception.

As always, the boys outnumbered the girls but there were enough of each to keep the elders from wondering about her choice in company.

"I was a good sermon, *yah?*" Rachel Bender said, trying to steer her away from the others as she tended to do, wanting Naomi all to herself. Yet Naomi did not allow herself to be led away, her green eyes glittering impishly as she took in her admirers. She had grown up with all of them, most having returned from Rumspringa with her only months earlier. Her interest in the boys far outweighed that of the girls.

"It is always a good sermon," Naomi conceded, her gaze training on Elijah Miller who returned her smile with one of his own. Of all her potential suitors, Elijah was winning her favor the most these days but that did not mean much in the grand scheme of things. Naomi was known to be fickle in her affections, a fact that was not lost on the other young men in her community.

It was not her fault. She liked all of her potential suitors. Each one of them had something of value to offer her but they all seemed to lack things as well. Naomi knew that she would not settle for anyone until she was sure she would have the perfect union.

"*Komme*, Naomi," Seth Eicher murmured, touching her arm brazenly as he realized that Elijah was her focus. "There are *schmierkees un lattwarrick*. I'll get you two."

"My *mudder* made those," Jacob Hooley interjected with annoyance, stepping forward from the group to set his own dark eyes on Naomi, who could barely contain her smug excitement at all the attention bestowed upon her. "If anyone should bring her a pastry, it's me."

The boys glowered at one another, and Naomi realized that it was time to diffuse the situation before matters grew too competitive.

"That sounds lovely," Naomi agreed, following Jacob toward the table where the morning's offerings had been laid out. She was careful not to fix too much energy on Elijah or any of the other men, lest they lose hope in winning her attentiveness. She had yet to decide who would be the lucky one she married, and she longed to keep her options open. In the interim, the boys were happy to trip over themselves for her eye and the girls were eager to keep their position as her friend. Even if she did not bestow the same energy upon the girls, Naomi was popular and well-liked. It was important to keep her amused.

The tables spread over the fields, the bright May sunshine overtaking the Smucker farm. All around them, the women hurried to lay out the offerings they had made at their own homes on that day of worship. Springtime had brought about the best in all the community, the men and women dressed in their Sunday finest, and the dark colors of winter forgotten in the wake of the fresh season. It was Naomi's favorite time of year, the smell of rebirth and greenness everywhere she walked.

She had barely taken two steps, the light blue hem of her newly stitched dress twirling at her ankles, when she heard her name called.

"Naomi."

The sound of her father's voice caused her to turn, her beam widening at the sight of her strapping papa. She had lost sight of him during the services, with the men separated to their side of the event, but now, she wondered how she might have not seen him. In her mind, he was the most handsome, hardest working man in all of the district, not one to be easily overlooked. Sometimes she wondered if that was not the reason she had yet to settle on a suitor. She would never find anyone quite as worthy as her father.

"*Hallo, Daed*," she said brightly. "Should I get you a plate? I hear there are special treats today."

To her surprise, Isaac Hershberger did not return her smile, a look of slight worry crossing his face. Isaac shook his graying head and ushered her to the side, away from the ears of her peers.

"*Nee*," he said with a slight sigh. "I need to discuss something with you. Will you give me a moment?"

Naomi's beam faltered slightly, and she nodded obediently as she waited for him to speak. She did not like to see Isaac with a frown, particularly not when the day was so beautiful. Whatever was troubling him was likely to be serious.

"Has something happened?" she asked with concern when Isaac did not speak immediately.

"*Nix*…well, not exactly," he muttered, looking at the grass below his feet as though he were trying to compose his thoughts. "I just overheard something that bothered me, and I thought it best to discuss it with you before it reaches your ears."

A fission of apprehension snaked down Naomi's spine. It was uncharacteristic of her father to speak so seriously. Since the passing of her mother, five years earlier, Isaac had made a great effort not to show upset or darkness in Naomi's presence. While Lydia's death had left a void in both their hearts, Isaac had been determined not to let his only daughter suffer the cloud of mourning that had brought so many other families down. He went out of his way to shower Naomi with affection and love, reminding her that there was endless beauty in the world, despite its sorrows. It was just one of the infinite reasons Naomi adored him so much.

"You can have anything you want in this life, Naomi," Isaac often told her. "And I will see that you get precisely that."

Naomi had always taken his reassurances to heart and now, as she was of age to marry, she intended to find the best that there was in her small world.

Which was why Isaac's demeanor was all the more unsettling.

"*Daed*, you're troubling me," she told him. "What is it?"

"I heard some of the women speaking in the *kucke*," he explained in a rush of breath. "They're concerned about you."

Naomi's dark blonde eyebrows shot up so quickly, they nearly touched her honey-brown hair.

"Which women? Who?"

Isaac waved his hand dismissively.

"That's not important," he said but Naomi thought otherwise. If it was important enough for Isaac to be worried, it was important for Naomi to know. She did not say those words and instead asked another question.

"Concerned about me?" she echoed with an amused laugh. "What could they possibly be worried about?"

"There were several topics of gossip," Isaac confessed. Naomi's neck stiffened and she eyed her father warily.

They talk about me? What could they possibly have to talk about? I am what every daughter should be! They would be lucky to have such a child. All their daughters want to be me!

"For one, you never bring anything to worship," Isaac said and sighed, flushing slightly.

"*Wat?*" Naomi sputtered in genuine confusion. "What does that mean?"

"You should bring something next *karrichdaag*," he rushed on. "Bread, a cake, something."

Naomi's face turned crimson. It had never occurred to her, despite the fact that she had watched the women bring food her entire life. The thought had simply not crossed her mind but now that Isaac was saying it aloud, Naomi was humiliated.

"It's not your fault," Isaac continued, seeing the look of defensiveness on her face. "Your *mudder* should have taught you that before... I mean, I should have been firmer on it but raising a girl is much more different than raising a boy..."

He cleared his throat with some embarrassment as he realized he was not vocalizing properly. Isaac paused to gather his thoughts while Naomi's jaw twitched but she wisely held her tongue on the matter.

"What else?" she asked dully.

"*Wat?*"

"What else did they have to say about me? There's more, isn't there?"

"Oh…" Isaac paused and again looked sheepishly at her, his pale green eyes, so much like her own, meeting hers evenly.

"*Daed*, you can tell me. I am grownup and can handle a bit of gossip."

Isaac seemed to weigh the words but still did not speak.

"*Daed…?*"

"They are not particularly fond of the way you won't choose a suitor," he blurted out. Naomi's mouth gaped open.

"What business is that of theirs?" she demanded, her voice raising angrily, but Isaac's gaze silenced her immediately. She looked about to see if anyone had heard but no one was paying her any mind except the group of impatient young men who waited a dozen feet away for her to join them.

"It is not their business," he conceded. "But you must admit that you should settle on someone. Half the boys in the district are falling all over themselves for you. The *wiewer*… well…they're worried about their sons and the games you might be playing with their affections."

Humiliation flooded Naomi's body and she struggled to find the words to speak but ultimately, she didn't say what she really wanted to.

The thought made her sick to her stomach. She had always seen herself as discerning. The fact that she had not committed to one man, or another should have been to her advantage, not her detriment. Naomi could barely believe what she was hearing.

"You're not in trouble, Mimi," he told her softly, reading the stricken expression on her face. "But you are a woman now and you must act like one."

Isaac offered her a patient smile, but he did not permit her a chance to respond.

"*Komme* and *esse*," he said, nodding toward the food but as he walked away to join the others, Naomi's thoughts were not on food. Her stomach felt as though there was a stone in its pit. She was not sure if she would ever eat again.

For a long moment, she could only stare after her father, her mind blank. Isaac did not look back, as though he could sense her upset and wished to run from it.

"*Hallo*, Naomi."

A pair of vivid blue eyes caught her attention and Naomi gasped when she looked up. She had not realized someone had been standing in her midst.

"I don't think you're doing anything wrong," Samuel Kropf said brightly. The sun shone on his bare, blonde hair, catching hints of white against its rays. A dimple appeared on his right cheek as he stared at her imploringly. His shy, awkward mannerisms infuriated Naomi, despite his startling attractiveness. She found his lack of confidence frustrating. More embarrassment shuddered through Naomi's body as she realized that Samuel had been listening in on the conversation between her and her father. She had not noticed him, no one noticed him. He tended to blend into the background.

"Are you alright?" Samuel pressed. "You look a bit pale. Should I fix you something to eat? They have a lot of food, and it's no trouble get you something. Whatever you like."

He was babbling but Naomi was stuck on his original statement.

"*Wat?*" she asked a little too tersely. "*Wat* did you say?"

Samuel blinked and stared at her.

"About *esse?*" he asked in confusion.

"You don't think I did what?" she growled.

"I-I don't think you're doing anything wrong," he reiterated, stepping closer. He towered over her by at least six inches, his lean frame blocking out the sun. Anger shot through her.

What do I care what he thinks? she thought, swallowing the lump of unhappiness in her throat. *He's no one important.*

Emboldened by her silence, Samuel continued.

"If you ask me, the *wiewer* have too much time on their hands if they're wasting their time gossiping about young *frau.*"

Naomi gawked at him, and Samuel returned her stare with guileless blue eyes.

"Nobody asked you!" she shot back. "Did anyone ask you to spy on us?"

"Well, no…" Samuel sputtered.

"What are you doing skulking about in the shadows?" she thundered at him. "Is this how you have your fun? Lurking around and listening in on private conversations? You're no better than the *haus frau* in the *kucke*! Maybe that's where they get their fodder! Maybe you're the one feeding them all this nonsense!"

Samuel's smiled faded at her harsh words and he stepped back as though he had been physically struck, his vivid eyes darkening. Naomi felt a stab of guilt as she heard the intensity of her words. She was not really angry at Samuel, but he was the only one there. She did not truly believe that he was gossiping about her.

Even if he were, who would listen to him?

"I-I wasn't spying…" he protested. Naomi grunted and spun around, the straps of her prayer bonnet smacking her in the mouth as she moved. She could feel him watching as she stormed away.

"I really wasn't!" Samuel cried out behind her, but Naomi did not turn back to acknowledge him. Her heart was pounding in her chest and consternation overwhelmed her. Even as her friends and admirers flocked around her again, Naomi could not manage a smile. She no longer knew who was talking about her while they grinned to her face.

In her mind, the perfectly lovely day had been ruined and a part of her hoped she had ruined Samuel Kropf's day too.

CHAPTER 2

*S*amuel watched as Naomi Hershberger all but stomped away without so much as a backward glance. He felt his heart swell with upset but it was not the first time he had been rebuked by Naomi, despite his best intentions to get closer to her.

For years, Samuel had admired the way Naomi carried herself through the district, her long hair and pretty green eyes captivating him at every glance. For as long as he could remember, he had followed after her, hoping for a glimpse of her or a smile from her.

But he was not a fool. Samuel understood that Naomi was coveted by many of the men in the community, but he had always held out hope that one day, she would see that he was just as worthy as Jacob Hooley or Elijah Miller. Yet as the months passed, his wishes faltered. It was clear that Naomi would think to even marry Seth Eicher with his clubbed foot and one lazy eye before giving Sam a chance. Or at least that was what his aunt Amity told him, trying to talk some sense into her only nephew.

"You will find a *gut frau* when *Gott* sees fit," Amity told Samuel in her stern, unemotional way. "You shouldn't go pining after the likes of Naomi Hershberger."

Samuel did not want to argue with his father's only sister. After all, Amity had been like a mother to him in many ways. She was certainly the only adult who had ever cared for him. His family had not been among the wealthier in their Amish community. Ever since Samuel had been born, he had known that Kropfs were unluckier than most.

His father had inherited a plot of land from his own father and had begun to build a small house upon it. Amity had married by then, leaving Abraham to run a farm with only his wife and very young son. Tirelessly, Abraham had worked, trying to finish the pretty building for his family and all had seemed to be going well when an early and unexpected tornado blew through their rural community and wiped out all that Abraham had built. His was the only building touched by the tornado, as though God had personally spoken and dictated that Abraham was not worthy of the house he had built.

Devastated and without any extra money to rebuild, Abraham had been forced to relocate his wife and child to Amity's house as he struggled to start over. Amity's husband, Daniel, had been less than accepting of the arrangement. The days and nights had been filled with arguments and strife, causing stress for everyone involved until Daniel gave his bride an ultimatum; Abraham and his family had to go.

Abraham used the church's resources where he could but with a useless plot of land and no house, he was falling deeper into despair. In the end, Abraham knew he needed to leave the district to find work, but Esther had not wanted to abandon her husband in his time of need.

From what Samuel recalled of those early days, there had been much shouting and sobbing, the tension running high in the house. The way Amity retold the tale, Esther had begged Abraham not to leave them behind, but her husband left for the city and Esther found the situation unbearable. Daniel was still not content, even though Abraham had left, and he separated from his wife, leaving the women alone in the house with a five-year-old Samuel.

Samuel's memory of the few months following was spotty. There had been a time when his mother disappeared for a while before returning, only to lock herself in the bedroom and refuse to eat or bathe. Amity had little choice but to care for a boy not her own as her sister-in-law sunk deeper and deeper into a depression.

It was Amity who found her sister-in-law, hanging from the rafters in the barn, a day before Samuel's sixth birthday.

For months, Samuel waited for his father to return but Abraham did not. It was not until Sam was much older that he realized Abraham had been shunned from the community. Samuel also discovered that Esther had left to look for her husband but had been unsuccessful. He often wondered how different his life would have been if his mother had found his father or if Abraham had taken his family with him when he left.

Daniel also did not return to the house, deciding instead to leave the state and start anew in another district. Amity was left with their small house and, while Bishop Troyer had ordered Daniel to pay her an allowance, he did not, leaving her to fend for herself.

Sometimes Samuel wondered if his aunt resented him for all that had happened, but she had never done anything but feed and clothe him until he was old enough to find his own work as a farmhand. It was nothing she outwardly said but he could not help but feel like there was a strain between them. Samuel was always cautious not to rock the boat with Amity—even when it had to do with something he felt as passionately about as Naomi Hershberger.

"You are not a child anymore, Samuel," Amity continued. "You must see that Naomi won't marry someone like you."

"Someone like me," Samuel sighed dully.

"You know exactly what I mean, Samuel."

And he did. He knew that Naomi Hershberger would look for a husband who was established, with land of his own. Someone handsome and confident. Someone exactly the opposite of Samuel.

She doesn't mean to be cruel. She's only speaking the truth I already know.

That did not mean it hurt any less hearing it from Amity's lips.

"What are you doing hiding here?"

His aunt's voice caused him to turn, and he tried to smile but the expression faltered terribly. Understanding instantly lit up in Amity's gray eyes. She sighed heavily.

"You will need to leave that girl alone. She's getting herself a reputation around here as it is."

For as much as Samuel felt the divide between himself and his aunt, he found it remarkable that she seemed to know him so well.

Defensiveness struck through Samuel's heart, but he managed to keep his feelings in check, again reminding himself that Amity meant well.

"You shouldn't pay any attention to the *haus fraus*," Samuel told her chidingly. "Once they were talking about you, in case you've forgotten."

A spark of annoyance shot through Amity's eyes as though she had forgotten and would have continued to forget if not for him. She changed the subject.

"Are you ready to leave? I promised Mrs. Tanner that I would have that dress ready for her tomorrow and I still have work to do."

Samuel nodded, not wanting to remind his aunt that she should not be working on a worship day. He knew all too well that every day was a struggle for her. Daniel had all but forsaken her in their once-shared house and now they scrounged for money. Samuel wouldn't tell anyone if his aunt, a seamstress, put in an extra couple of hours that afternoon. He was not sure he would refuse if one of his employers asked him to work on a Sunday, not that it was ever likely to happen. Samuel was eager to leave anyway. His ego had been substantially bruised by Naomi and no one would miss them if they skipped the meal and returned home.

"*Gut*," Amity said, spinning toward the front of the house where the buggies waited. Barely anyone acknowledged that they were leaving but that was commonplace. Samuel had always known that they were outsiders in the close-knit community. It made him sad and confused. He wanted nothing more than to be accepted but he could not force the community to embrace them.

Silently, he and Amity climbed aboard the buggy and headed the twenty minutes home. Samuel inhaled the smell of sweetgrass and hay as they moved, wishing that the fresh scent of spring would shake him from the dismal mood in which he found himself. He loved the spring. It represented a time of newness and starting over. Every March, he found himself thinking that the new season would bring with it change, both in himself and among his peers.

Particularly with Naomi.

"What is it you see in her? Samuel?" Amity asked suddenly, shattering Samuel's depressive reverie. "She treats you so poorly. Time and again, I have seen you like this, crushed by her words and actions."

He cast his aunt a sidelong look, knowing that the question was rhetorical, but it made him question his feelings yet again.

Perhaps it had always been her beauty that had drawn him to Naomi, but he was certain there was more to it than that. There were plenty of lovely girls in the district, some of whom were much kinder to Sam than Naomi.

But none of them are Naomi. There is goodness in her heart, no matter how she lashes out at me. I can see it or else I wouldn't think she is so beautiful.

That was not something he could easily explain to his cynical aunt and if he tried, he would only end up fumbling the words and solidifying her belief that Naomi was not worthy of the love he had for her.

"I don't know," he finally answered, honestly. "I have always loved her."

Amity grunted rudely and turned her head to stare at the landscape, only the white of her prayer bonnet facing Sam's view.

"You don't know about *lieb*," she grumbled slightly. "You have puppy lust for her. You are a man now, Samuel, too old to be following that girl around like a lost *hund*."

Again, Samuel felt indignation rising inside him, but he shoved it aside. There was no point in arguing with Amity. She had always been set in her ways; her convictions carved in stone.

"I know you think you love her," Amity went on even though Samuel did not speak. "But if you did, you would accept what is."

Samuel turned his head, his fingers inadvertently tightening around the reins as he met Amity's gaze. For a moment, he thought he caught a shimmer of sadness, but it was gone before he could be certain.

Amity is too cold to feel sadness.

"I have accepted what is," he replied slowly. "How have I not?"

"You haven't because you continue to chase her," Amity replied, sounding annoyed that she had to explain it. "If you truly cared about her, you would let *Gott* lead your path and allow her to be happy with someone else. *Gott* has spoken but you are deaf to His words. This will only lead to more heartache and a question of your own faith down the line."

The words hit Samuel with a slap, and he blinked at the reality of it. He had never looked at the situation like that before. His desires had clouded his judgement and he found himself wondering if his aunt was right.

She's not wrong, he thought, slowing moving his eyes back to the road in front of them. *I should have faith in His plan. If that means that Naomi ends up with another man, I will have to accept that is Gott's will.*

Pain like he had never felt before gripped at Samuel's heart but with it came a sense of knowledge that Amity had spoken the truth. Another long, uncomfortable silence fell between them, Samuel slipping back into his dark place when his aunt spoke again.

"Samuel, I only mean to steer you away from hurt and heartache," Amity murmured in a voice so low that he barely heard it. He strained to listen more. "I would not want anyone to endure what I have gone through, especially not the only *familye* I have left."

Samuel swallowed the lump that had formed in his throat, feeling the burn of disappointment in his eyes but somehow, he managed to keep himself from displaying any of what he was feeling.

"I understand, Amity," he told her, hearing the catch of his own voice. "And you're right. I should not question *Gott* or His plan. Whoever Naomi marries; I will accept with grace."

He did not miss the look of dubiousness on Amity's face, as if she did not believe that Samuel would be able to let go of the matter so easily, but her expression only hardened his resolve.

"I only want Naomi to be happy," he told her honestly. "If it is not with me, I pray that she finds a good husband that will give her a good life. That *is* what love is, isn't it?"

He did not add that he was thinking he knew he was the best possible choice for Naomi, no matter what she believed. There would never be any man who could love her as well as he could. The only problem was he could never get close enough to Naomi to prove it to her.

"You're a good boy, Sam." Amity sighed, an unexpected tenderness in her tone. "You deserve better than Naomi Hershberger."

Sam managed a small, mirthless smile but as they fell back into a deep silence, he knew that was not true. He and Naomi belonged together, even if she could not see it. He did not deserve better because there was no better.

He only hoped that Naomi might come to her senses before she made any decisions on her future without him, but he was not going to hold his breath, not anymore.

CHAPTER 3

aomi had not wanted to attend the cattle auction with her father, her ego still dented from the insult she had received on Sunday at worship. She had spent the past three days close to the house and away from gossiping lips as she tried to make sense of what her father had told her. She wanted to press him more on who the women were, but she knew Isaac well enough to know that he would not tell her, lest she confront them for their chatter.

It doesn't matter what anyone has to say about me, she told herself over and over. *I will make my own decisions when the time is right. I don't care what they talk about.*

Yet she knew that was not true. In a community like theirs, it was impossible to ignore, and Naomi felt herself slipping into a slight depression. It was a daunting feeling, one that was foreign and uncomfortable. Naomi had always been a happy girl. This was unusual behavior for her.

Perhaps that was the reason that Isaac had been insistent, even if he did not rouse the topic of what had happened again throughout the week.

"Are you ready to go?" he asked from the doorway of her bedroom. She blinked and stared at him.

"Go where?" she demanded in confusion. Isaac sighed.

"The cattle auction is today. Don't tell me you forgot."

She had forgotten but that did not matter.

"I'm not going," she said, cinching her braid with an elastic and tucking it under the base of her skull.

"What do you mean?" Isaac inquired. "Of course, you are."

"*Nee*, I'm not," Naomi said flatly. The thought of leaving the house was too much at that moment.

"I need you at my side," Isaac told her. "You have a better eye for the livestock than I do."

"*Daed*, I have work to do at the *haus*," she pleaded weakly, knowing that was not the real reason for her hesitation. "Can't you go on your own this one time?"

"I can," Isaac agreed. "But I don't want to. What if I pick the wrong *kuh*? You'll never let me hear the end of it."

Naomi gaped at him.

"That's not true!"

"I don't want to find out," Isaac said sternly. "Hurry up and get dressed. I'll wait for you."

He turned to return to the main floor, but Naomi called out again one last time in desperation.

"*Daed…*"

"*Wat?*"

"You can do it without me," Naomi grumbled but, in the end, her father had left her little choice and the pair headed into Reading for the affair. Usually, Naomi enjoyed these outings. While she had no desire to live outside the district, she did like to watch the Englishers and the way they interacted with one another. Moreover, it gave Naomi an opportunity to meet other Amish families from other parts of the county—particularly eligible young men.

Yet that day, she was feeling disheartened and when they took a seat outside among the auctioneers, Naomi barely noticed the other people around them. The sun shone hotly above but a slight breeze broke up the potential for overheating. Even so, Naomi could not bring herself to appreciate the beauty around her.

"You're acting sullen," Isaac chided her. "What is it?"

She did not admit to him that she was still in a bad mood and instead forced a smile.

"I'm not sullen," she argued.

"You haven't smiled in days," he complained. "Does this have anything to do with what happened on *Karrichdaag*?"

Baffled that he was being so blunt, Naomi flushed and shook her head in denial.

He hasn't asked me about that since it happened, and he chooses now to rouse the topic?

She knew why. There was less of a chance for a long discussion on the matter in such a public forum.

Daed is infuriatingly clever.

"I had forgotten all about that," she fibbed. If they were to discuss it, it was not going to be there. Isaac did not look convinced but turned his attention toward the front where the auctioneer was setting up. She was relieved that he had decided not to pursue it.

"We don't need to stay long," Isaac assured her. "A steer or two and maybe a few cows."

"*Yah, Daed,*" Naomi agreed but as she spoke, her eyes fell upon a tall, young man that she had never seen before. A familiar spark of interest peaked inside Naomi when she studied his physique, marveling at his height and long, dark curls.

Who is that?

Suddenly, all her misgivings and grumpiness dissipated like a wisp of smoke. From where she sat, Naomi could see that the stranger was very attractive and the realization that she did not know him intrigued her more. He turned abruptly as though he could feel her watching him and Naomi's breath was stolen at the sheer blue of his eyes. Even from the distance between them, she could make out the intensity of his stare. A slow, curious beam formed on his lips, the corners of his clean-shaven face twitching.

And he's not married!

The odds that there was a handsome and eligible young man in the district that she had not met were astronomical.

Where has he been all this time? Is he new to Lancaster County?

Naomi intended to find out. Nervously, she looked about for an excuse to go near him. She could feel the young man watching her with amused curiosity.

"Excuse me, *Daed*," Naomi mumbled, rising from her spot before her father could stop her. "I need to find some *wasser*."

"Now?" Isaac protested. "The auction is about to begin!"

"I'm thirsty," Naomi fibbed, gathering her skirt and shifting her way up the row, past the other auction goers.

"Hurry back!" Isaac called out after her, but Naomi barely heard him. She was drawn to the stranger like a magnet and without shame or bashfulness, she made her way to his side. He did not seem surprised to see her, as though he had summoned her over with his mind.

"*Hallo*," Naomi breathed as he turned to face her fully, his grin widening appreciatively. His crystalline eyes were even more startling up close, and Naomi felt her heart flutter. Everything about his face was exquisite.

"*Hallo*, Naomi Hershberger," he replied, startling her as she gawked at him in shock.

"You know my name?" she asked, half-pleased, half-surprised. Her mind raced for where she might have met him, but Naomi was certain she would have remembered him under any circumstance. She had never laid eyes on him before.

"*Yah*, of course," he chuckled. "Everyone knows the name of the most beautiful woman in Lancaster County."

He paused and cocked his head to the side, his straw hat slipping slightly over his silken head of hair.

"You don't know my name though, do you?"

Embarrassment colored Naomi's cheeks and she shook her head, looking down at her feet.

"I-I don't think I do."

She could read the open disappointment on his face, and she was ashamed of herself for admitting it aloud.

"Josiah Wenger. I live in the district next to yours. Our fathers do business together sometimes."

Naomi had no idea. Inadvertently, she glanced behind her to look at Isaac, but he was distracted with the program in his hands.

Daed knows this man and never introduced me? How could he?

Naomi vowed to demand answers of her father later. She turned back to fix her full attention on Josiah.

"Oh…" Naomi offered him a flirtatious smile. "Well, it's very nice to meet you, Josiah."

Again, she was confused as to how they might not have met. She wracked her mind to remember a time when she might have chanced upon this attractive young man, but she was drawing a blank, much to her increasing humiliation. She wondered why her father had not thought to introduce them.

Maybe I have been spending too much time with too many other boys, she thought, her ears turning pink at the memory of what the women had said. *I'm missing out on better things by casting too wide of a net.*

"The pleasure is mine, Naomi," Josiah said, increasing the heat shooting through her slender frame. She felt vulnerable under his piercing stare, but she could not look away from the lovely blue of his eyes.

"Have you come for the auction?" Naomi asked, feeling foolish at the question as it left her lips. There was no other reason for him to be there, after all. To her relief, Josiah merely nodded.

"*Yah.* We need some more livestock for our *bauerei,*" he conceded. "We come once a month. We go through cattle far too quickly, it seems."

Naomi looked around to see who else he had in his company, but she could not determine if he had come with another. There were certainly no women among them and that ignited another ray of hope inside Naomi.

"I think your *vadder* is getting upset," Josiah offered, nodding toward where Isaac sat. Naomi turned and saw her father's narrowed eyes as he shook his head reprovingly. Naomi sighed.

"I should get back to him," she agreed, regret fueling her words. She had only just found this handsome man and she was not sure if she would ever see him again. As if reading her mind, Josiah brazenly touched her arm. A bolt of energy sparked through her at the touch and Naomi blinked in disbelief. She did not withdraw and instead tilted her head back in wonderment to gaze at his face.

"If you like, I can drive you home after the auction," he said boldly. "We could talk then."

Naomi blinked at the blunt offer, but her heart swelled with excitement.

"I-I would have to ask my *vadder*," she told him, but she was sure that Isaac would permit it. If their fathers did business together, Isaac would be more open to the idea. Josiah's mouth curved into a beam of happiness, and he nodded.

"All right," he conceded, releasing her arm but Naomi could still feel the heat of his touch against her skin, and it gave her shivers. "If he accepts, I'll be by the entrance, waiting for you afterward."

Naomi nodded, not trusting her voice but as she moved away, she instantly locked eyes on Samuel Kropf who stood a few feet away with his employer's other farmhands. For an odd moment, Naomi's happiness was stolen, the look of pure anguish on Samuel's face penetrating to her very core. Palpable waves of hurt seemed to emanate from his eyes. In spite of her resolve to ignore him, Naomi could not help but feel a sense of shame.

Don't be silly, she snapped at herself, pulling her eyes away from the blond man and moving quickly toward where her father was sat. *It's not my fault that I don't have feelings for Samuel. I haven't done anything wrong. He should stop pining after me so blatantly. I'm embarrassed for him.*

Yet as she settled at Isaac's side, she could not shake the sensation that she might have handled herself better with a man who so clearly adored her. The memory of how she had spoken to him on Sunday was still fresh in her mind. She idly thought of apologizing to him, but she quickly dismissed the thought.

Surely, he should know better than to lurk around and listen to other people's conversations.

"Did you get your *wasser*?" Isaac asked dryly when she reclaimed her seat at his side. Naomi giggled; her cheeks still pink.

"*Nee*," she replied honestly. "Do you know that young man?"

"He's Amos Wenger's boy, *yah*?"

Hope overrode all of Naomi's doubts and Samuel Kropf was forgotten.

"Josiah, *yah*," Naomi conceded. "Why haven't you ever introduced us?"

Isaac seemed perplexed by the question.

"I can't say," he said slowly but in such a way that made Naomi think he was hiding something. She hesitated but Isaac, knowing his daughter too well spoke for her.

"Has he asked you to do something?"

Naomi blushed. Her head was beginning to ache with all the emotion coursing through her mind.

"He's asked to take me home after the auction," she admitted. "I told him that it would depend on your answer."

She let the statement hang between them, but Isaac pondered the idea with more thought than Naomi expected.

"They are a *gut familye*," he agreed after a moment. "I see no harm in him escorting you home."

Relief shot through Naomi, although she was not sure what other outcome she had anticipated.

Daed would like to see me married soon also, she reasoned, eying him through her peripheral vision. *He approves of Josiah.*

Her head rose and her gaze met with Josiah who had been watching from across the lawn. She nodded vehemently to indicate that their ride was happening, and he grinned broadly. But as Naomi again moved her eyes back to the auctioneer, her stare paused on the naked sadness of Samuel's face. He quickly looked away, but it ruined Naomi's fleeting happiness all the same.

He will need to move on with his life, she thought firmly. *His pain is not my problem.*

She wished that she did not feel so guilty in spite of her own reassurances.

CHAPTER 4

As promised, Josiah was waiting for Naomi near the exit as the auction came to a close. He seemed almost impatient as Isaac escorted his daughter to the young man's waiting buggy.

"You'll take her straight *deheem*, *yah*?" Isaac asked Josiah pointedly. "No stops along the way?"

"*Yah*," Josiah agreed. "I have to get home also. My *mudder* is waiting."

Isaac held Josiah's gaze a moment longer than necessary and Naomi swallowed a smile, knowing that her father was making his authority known.

He's such a good vadder. I am blessed to have him.

"May we go, *Daed*?" Naomi pressed when the stare went on to uncomfortable lengths. Isaac seemed content with Josiah's promise and nodded.

"All right then. I want you to go straight home," he reiterated.

"*Yah, Daed*. I heard you," Naomi tittered. The men helped Naomi onto the buggy. Relief washed though her when she saw that her father approved of the young man and the two left Isaac to pay for the cattle he had purchased.

Naomi was very aware of Josiah's nearness and caught herself studying his face openly as they rode through the simple country roads, toward Ephrata. Suddenly, the glory of the day was all that Naomi could feel, the sun's rays warming her to her very soul. Her mood had taken a hundred and eighty degree turn from how she had arrived at the auction.

I will never fight with Daed again about going anywhere, she promised herself. Naomi knew that her newfound happiness had less to do with the sun and everything to do with Josiah's presence, but Naomi basked in the sensation all the same.

"Are you very close to Ephrata?" she asked, stirring up the conversation between them.

"I live closer to New Holland," Josiah explained. "But not that far away from you at all. Only twenty-five minutes."

His words were laced with promise and Naomi could barely hide her smile. The fact that he had timed the distance between their houses already made her pulse race.

He is just as interested in me as I am in him, she though happily.

"That is *gut* to know," she said softly, raising her eyes toward him. "You have a cattle farm like us?"

"My *vadder* has two businesses," Josiah explained. "We have a small cattle farm, but his main trade is woodworking. That is what he prefers to do but the cattle are supplemental."

Naomi was impressed. The Wengers were well-established, it seemed.

Handsome, hard-working, charming... what else could I possibly ask for in a future husband?

For the first time, Naomi found herself fully invested in the possibility that she might have found the man she had sought for so long. She dared not let herself get too excited, but it was impossible to dismiss the mounting glee inside her.

"That must be a lot of work for you," she said, eying him. Josiah shrugged.

"There are eight *kinner* in the *haus*. My sisters take care of the *haus* and the livestock, mostly. My brothers and I work in the shop. It is not too much when everyone knows their place."

And he comes from a large familye! He only gets better with each word!

"Even so, you must be very busy," she commented. Josiah cast her a sidelong look.

"Not so busy that I can't focus on my own *familye* when we're married."

Naomi laughed at his wording, her stomach fluttering. She knew that he must have misspoken but she liked the way it had sounded. However, Josiah did not smile.

"What's so funny?" he asked, sounding confused. "Don't you want to get married?"

"Of course," she replied, beaming so broadly her cheeks hurt. "Doesn't everyone?"

"*Nee*, Naomi, I mean get married to me. I'm talking about our wedding."

The smile on Naomi's face froze and she realized he was being serious.

"*Yah*, of course I want to get married," she replied slowly, her breath catching slightly as she struggled to understand how this stranger could be talking about getting married already.

"We could announce our intention by the fall," Josiah continued, and the smile fully slipped off Naomi's face. The magic of the afternoon was fizzling slightly.

"Josiah…" she faltered. "I-I hardly know you."

His brow furrowed and he cast her a sidelong look, his eyes still on the road ahead.

"Our *familye* know each other," he said. "Your *vadder* and mine. We're having a *gut* time, aren't we?"

Dumbfounded, Naomi could only stare at him, unsure of what to say.

"I have waited a long time to find the right woman to marry," Josiah continued. "My *familye* is established in the district and we have a lot of land. Our businesses are doing well."

"I-I'm sure that's all true," Naomi stammered. "That doesn't change the fact that I don't know you."

"What is it you need to know?" Josiah pressed. "You can ask me anything and I'll tell you. Go ahead."

Naomi blinked, not liking the sudden turn of events. She felt put on the spot, uncomfortable, but Josiah did not seem to think there was anything wrong with the way he was behaving.

"Well? What would you like to ask me?" he pressed.

"I don't know exactly…" she murmured, looking down at her hands. "But I'm sure there is more to know than what a half hour buggy ride can tell me."

A long, uncomfortable silence followed her words and Naomi worried that she had ruined her opportunity before it had even truly begun. She wracked her brain with what to say to make it better but in the end, she could think of nothing. Agreeing to marry a near-stranger was not something she was willing to do but she considered that she might be letting go of the one man she had been seeking for years.

"All right," Josiah said, breaking their awkward quiet with a resigning sigh. "I'm willing to wait until you think you know me better."

Naomi's heart exploded and a rush of dizziness made her heady. It was all she could do to keep from squealing with delight.

"Really?" she choked. "You will?"

"I have watched you from afar for a long while, Naomi and I'm sure that we will end up married, but if you're not sure, I can't force you."

He did not sound happy about it, but Naomi was ecstatic that she had not lost him, despite her reservations.

"I just need a little bit of time," she told him confidently. "A proper courtship."

A wry smile touched the corners of Josiah's mouth and he nodded begrudgingly.

"I can give you that," he agreed. Naomi's shoulders sank with relief, and she turned her head toward the landscape, sure that her cheeks were as red as autumn apples.

Of course, he wouldn't rush me, she thought, feeling silly that she had worried at all. *Any man that would do that is not worthy of my hand.*

She snuck another look at Josiah and beamed widely.

Denki Gott, she thought gratefully. *Denki for sending me Josiah.*

NAOMI WAS PREPARING supper when Isaac finally returned from the auction.

"How was your drive with Josiah?" he asked, a knowing smile twitching on his lips. Naomi was bursting to tell her father all about the young man.

"He seems wonderful, *Daed,*" she confessed in a rush of breath. "I think he is everything I have wanted in a *mann.*"

Isaac's eyebrows shot up in surprise.

"A *mann, yah?*" There was a wisdom in his words, as if he had already suspected his daughter was smitten with Josiah.

"I mean... well, I don't know him yet," she mumbled, realizing that she was putting the cart before the horse. "But from what I've seen..."

Isaac chuckled.

"I am happy to hear you finally setting your sights on someone in particular, Naomi. You'll leave so many of the other young men disappointed. Be sure before you fully commit to anyone, *yah*?"

Unexpectedly, Naomi thought of Samuel Kropf and his soulful eyes watching her at the auction.

"I haven't made any promises to anyone," she said quickly, turning back to tend to the roast.

"It sounds like you may have," Isaac replied dryly.

"I haven't," Naomi insisted but she could hear her own uncertainty. After that afternoon, there was little doubt that she and Josiah had a future together. Their attraction was undeniable.

I shouldn't fight this. Gott has spoken to us both. He has been waiting just as long as I have to find the right partner. I won't make Josiah fight for me like I have the others.

"Is *nachtesse* almost ready?" Isaac asked, slipping Naomi out of her reverie. She nodded.

"It will be in ten minutes."

Isaac nodded and moved out of the kitchen to wash up for supper, leaving his daughter to ponder his words.

If all goes well with Josiah, we could be announcing our intention to marry by the fall, as he suggested.

The happiness she felt was unlike anything she had ever known before. It was as if she was floating on a cloud, one that Isaac instantly picked up on when he returned from the second floor to sit at the dining room table.

"I must say, I'm surprised," he confessed when his daughter laid out their meal and they had said their prayers.

"Surprised about what?"

"Josiah Wenger never struck me as the type to settle down," he explained. The comment took the wind out of Naomi's sails slightly.

"What do you mean?"

Isaac paused to chew the potatoes in his mouth before replying.

"To be honest, his *vadder* was stunned he returned to be baptized after Rumspringa."

Naomi stared at him, a slight apprehension snaking through her.

"But he is *daafe*, isn't he?" she asked worriedly. "He is baptized?"

"*Ach yah, yah,*" Isaac reassured her. "I wouldn't have let you go off with him otherwise."

Naomi sat back and looked at her plate.

"Then he must be committed to the Ordnung," she said slowly, wondering if she was trying to convince herself or her father.

"Of course, he is," Isaac said, eying her warily. "Oh… I didn't mean to give you any doubts, Mimi. He seems very taken with you."

Naomi quickly dismissed the idle suspicions trying to sneak into her mind and she claimed her fork to join her father in their evening meal.

After supper, Isaac retired to the front room and Naomi her own, going up early after the day's events. She was emotionally tired from all that she had experienced, and her body welcomed the softness of her mattress as she slipped between the sheets.

Closing her eyes, Naomi expected to see Josiah's face appear behind her lids but once more, she was plagued by the desolate expression of Samuel Kropf.

Her eyes instantly reopened.

Why do I keep thinking about him? she wondered with annoyance but as she again closed her eyes and Samuel's face reappeared, Naomi wondered whether this was a message from God.

He wants me to pray for Samuel, Naomi realized, accepting the vision as it came now. *Gott knows that Samuel pines for me but that we can never be. I must pray that he finds a frau who makes him happy.*

She was not plagued with the usual irritation she felt whenever she thought of Samuel, and she knew that was because she had found joy in Josiah's company.

I want Samuel and everyone else to know this same feeling, she thought honestly. Naomi said a silent prayer for Samuel in her head, but her heart was still fixated on Josiah. She could hardly wait for what the upcoming days had to bring.

CHAPTER 5

*A*s Naomi had predicted, the next few days far exceeded her expectations. Josiah came to call on her every day with a small bunch of flowers each time.

"There is a field near my house," he explained on the third day as he handed her the simple bouquet. "My sister, Sarah, picks them daily."

The information was bittersweet. Naomi had hoped that Josiah picked them himself, but she did not comment on it. The fact that he thought to bring them at all was good enough.

"They are beautiful," she told him as they walked along the road. The sun was still over the horizon, but the evening was settling in as the days grew longer. It would soon be summer, and their time together would be extended as darkness held off. "I'd like to see your house soon."

Josiah offered her one of his charming smiles.

"I was holding off on bringing you there until I could tell my *mudder* the good news," he said.

"The good news?" Naomi echoed, confused. "What is it?"

His smile wilted slightly.

"Our betrothal, I mean."

"Oh." Naomi giggled lightly but this time, she was not as stunned by his words as she had been when he had first suggested it. She had given the idea of marriage to Josiah a lot of thought and she knew now that they were put on the same path for a reason.

"You seem more open to the idea," Josiah said slowly, stopping to face her. Hope shone in his eyes. "Are you warming up to the notion."

Naomi swallowed the thickness in her throat. She nodded slowly, not trusting her voice.

"I knew it!" Josiah cheered gleefully, wrapping his arms around her waist. "I knew you would come to your senses!"

A spark of irritation slid down Naomi's neck.

I had never lost my senses, she thought but she did not speak her mind. Josiah's nearness made her forget her annoyance and she looked up into his eyes. Suddenly, she realized how close they were, and she untangled herself from his hold. Josiah released her instantly.

"I'll talk to Bishop Troyer in the *mariye*," Josiah told her excitedly. "We can start making plans. We might not even need to wait until the fall."

"Wait!" Naomi laughed, holding up a hand. "I haven't agreed to anything."

"Maybe not with your words," Josiah countered, grinning unabashedly. "But I can see it in your eyes."

The sky turned a smoky pink and Naomi raised her head to look at the fading light.

"We should get back to the *haus*," she told him. "I don't want my *vadder* to worry."

Josiah did not argue and followed Naomi as she turned back the way they had come.

"And what does Isaac think about us getting married?" Josiah asked, a teasing lilt to his voice.

"What makes you think I've discussed such a thing with him?" Naomi replied coyly. Josiah laughed.

"I feel as if I've known you my whole life already, Naomi," he told her. "But if you won't tell me, I'll have to ask him myself."

With that, Josiah broke into a run toward the Hershberger property, leaving Naomi stunned.

"Wait for me!" she yelled, laughing as she snatched up the hem of her skirt and sprinted after him. She was out of breath by the time she caught up with him, turning the corner to walk up the long driveway.

"I'm going to ask him!" Josiah taunted, turning to smile at her as he danced backward. "He's going to—"

Josiah's words died on his lips as a look of horror crossed over Naomi's face.

"Mimi?"

Unable to speak, Naomi extended a finger and pointed behind him. Before Josiah could spin about to look, she took off in the direction of the barn.

Smoke billowed out from the half-open doors, the livestock mooing restlessly as they backed away. Flames licked out of the shattered windows.

"Mimi, don't!" Josiah yelled as she sprinted closer. Her eyes fell on the well and in seconds, she rushed to fill a bucket. Strong arms seized her and forced her back as water sloshed over the ground.

"Just leave it!" Josiah cried. "I'll go for help."

She looked helplessly at the blazing building, knowing that the water in her hands was not apt to do anything but before she could concede, she heard a faint cry.

"*HILF! HILF* ME!"

Dread and consternation overwhelmed Naomi as she realized it was her father's voice.

"*DAED!*" she screamed, whirling around to look at Josiah. "My *vadder* is in there!"

She moved to run forward but Josiah held her back.

"There's nothing you can do," he said firmly.

Shocked at his refusal to help, Naomi wrenched herself out of Josiah's grasp and rushed toward the burning barn.

"*ICH BIN OM COOMA, DAED*!" she howled against the roaring flames, but her voice was drowned out as she threw open the door. A blast of hot, smoky air assaulted her face and Naomi paused, choking on the cinders as she tried to get her bearings. "*DAED*!"

"*NEE NAOMI*!" Isaac howled. "Get out! Get back!"

His words gave her a sense of direction and armed with the bucket of water, she fought through the haze toward him. She finally caught a glimpse of him, trapped in one of the stalls, surrounded by burning wood. Without hesitation, Naomi sprung forward and doused the flames.

"*Komme*! Hurry!"

Isaac shot forward out of the stall and made his way toward the doors, his hand extended toward his daughter. She lunged forward to take it but as she did, there was a terrible groan from above. Instinctively, Naomi shoved her father away, just as the flaming beam came crashing down.

It was the last thing she recalled before the world went dreadfully black.

THE ANGELS MURMURED, their voices a blur in Naomi's mind. She could hear them whispering.

"*Gott*?" she mumbled but the mere word sent her scratchy throat into a dry spell of coughs.

"Mimi! Oh!"

Her eyes fluttered open weakly, and the sight of her father's concerned face sent Naomi's stomach into flips. Instantly, she recalled her last waking moments and struggled to sit up.

"*Nee*! Mimi, *nee*, you must not move," Isaac whispered, gently pushing her back toward the bed and Naomi realized that she was in her own room.

"*Daed*, are you hurt?" she sputtered when her coughs died down. As she spoke, an abrupt, searing pain shot through her face and she blinked uncomprehendingly. Her hand rose to touch her cheek but before she could make contact, her father stopped her, grabbing her wrist.

"Don't," he said with more force than she had ever heard him use. Startled, she looked at him in disbelief.

"Here, *liebling*."

Naomi turned her head at the sound of a woman's voice. Ruth Adler stood at her side, a glass of water extended in her hands.

"Drink this," the neighbor said kindly. Warily, she accepted the offering, her eyes trailing back toward her father who had released her arm and looked away. When she had finished, she spoke again.

"*Daed*, are you hurt?" she asked again. For the first time in her life, Naomi saw tears fill her father's eyes and the sight sent her into a panic.

"*Daed*, what happened?" she whispered but Isaac could not look at her. Terror gripped her heart and she again attempted to sit up, but a wave of dizziness overcame her, and she fell back.

"The *doktor* said that the pills would make her disoriented," Ruth murmured. "Not too much now, Isaac. It's more than she can bear."

Confusion overwhelmed Naomi and she began to cry.

"*Nee, nee*," Isaac said, sitting on the bed to take her hands. "Don't cry, *liebling*. Everything will be all right, you'll see."

"Why won't you tell me what happened?" Naomi sobbed.

"Shh, now," Isaac said, eying Ruth who hung her head heavily. "Do you remember the fire?"

"*Yah*, of course!" Naomi cried, sniffling. "How could I forget that?"

"You were so brave, Mimi," he told her tenderly. "You raced to save me without any thought to your own safety."

"Were you safe?" she demanded imploringly. "You are acting so strangely."

"I was not hurt, thanks to you," Isaac said. As he spoke, the pain in her face became more acute and Naomi gasped, intuitively moving to touch it but as she did, Isaac again snatched her hand away.

"I was not hurt," he continued. "But you were. Quite badly."

Dazed, Naomi could only stare at him, wondering what he was saying.

"I... how?" she whispered but as she asked the question, she had a terrible sense of foreboding that she already knew the answer.

"My face..."

Isaac lowered his eyes and nodded.

"The burns to your face are bad," he murmured. "Very bad."

Gasping, Naomi pulled herself up and looked about for a mirror.

"Mimi—" Isaac started to say but she cut him off.

"I need a mirror," she choked.

"*Nee*. That's not a good idea—"

"NOW!"

Never in her life had Naomi roared so loudly or with so much ferocity but she did not regret it. She had to see what had become of her face. Ruth looked awkwardly at Isaac, and he nodded, anguish painted over his expression.

A moment later, Ruth returned with a hand-held vanity mirror and put it to Naomi's face. Inhaling, the younger woman opened her eyes.

She barely recognized herself with the gaunt eyes and pale face. Part of her long hair had been singed off and a white gauze covered her left side. Her fingers moved toward the bandage and Ruth tried to argue but Isaac held up his hand for her be silent.

"She should see," Isaac said with a sigh, unable to look for himself.

Slowly, Ruth peeled the wrapping away from her face, her heart racing dangerously as she did.

"Oh!"

A fresh batch of tears welled in her eyes, and she gasped in horror at the sight. She looked like a gruesome figure that the Englisch used to decorate their lawns during Halloween. The skin had been peeled away, to what appeared to be almost the bone, exposing the red raw tissue below her cheekbone, clear to her chin.

"*Nee…*" Naomi whispered. "I-I can't live like this."

"There are doctors and medicines that can heal this," Ruth told her comfortingly, but the words fell flatly in Naomi's ears.

"It is a fresh wound," Isaac offered. "It will get better. It will heal."

"There will be a scar," Naomi insisted, throwing the mirror aside onto the bed. Bile rose to her throat and before she could stop herself, she vomited over the blanket.

"*Lieb*, it will be all right," Isaac said soothingly. "*Gott* spared your life and that is the most important thing."

"Josiah!"

She remembered him for the first time and panic seized her.

"Where is Josiah?"

Perplexed, Isaac and Ruth looked at one another.

"Josiah?" Isaac echoed. "H-he came by this morning. I can send for him…"

He trailed off as though he wanted to say more but thought better of it. Memories of Josiah and his refusal to help flooded back in a torrent.

"Does he know?" she breathed. "Does he know what's happened to my face?"

A long, foreboding silence followed her question.

"Why did you tell him?" Naomi wailed, throwing her head back against the pillows. "He won't want me like this! No one will ever want me like this!"

"Mimi, you can't think of anything but recovery right now," Isaac told her firmly.

"No," Naomi said suddenly, shaking her head. "Josiah will love me anyway. He is a *gut* man. He says *Gott* has put us together and it's true. We'll still be married."

"The *doktor* has given you something for the pain," Isaac said, quickly changing the subject. "Your mind isn't clear right now. We'll talk more after you've rested."

"*Daed?*" she murmured.

"*Yah, liebling?*"

"Will you tell Josiah I'm awake?"

"Of course, Mimi."

"Will you go now?"

"*Nee*, Mimi. You need to rest, and your risk of infection runs high. We can't have too many people here or it endangers you."

Naomi opened her mouth to protest but she could tell that arguing would only prove futile.

"Rest and I'll make you some *supp*," Ruth promised, leading Isaac out of the room before Naomi could say another word. As the door closed in their wake, Naomi had never felt so alone.

Everything will work itself out. Josiah will be here soon, and this nightmare will be done with.

CHAPTER 6

*I*saac had been reluctant to allow Naomi to go to the market.

"You should continue to rest," he told her worriedly. "You need sleep to heal."

"*Daed*, I have been locked in the *haus* for two weeks," Naomi complained. "I am going *verrickt* staying home all the time."

There was more to her reasoning than mere boredom. Naomi suspected that Isaac had purposely kept Josiah from visiting while she recovered, and she had heard a rumor through Ruth that the Wengers were opening a furniture store in the district soon. Naomi privately hoped that she might see Josiah, if only to let him know that she had missed him dearly. She was sure that he would feel the same.

"Mimi, there's nothing in town for you," Isaac insisted but he inadvertently looked at her scarred cheek and flushed. A slight humiliation shot through Naomi, and she frowned.

"Are you concerned that people will talk about my face?" she demanded. "You heard what the *doktor* said. It will continue to get better."

She was not sure how much faith of her own she put into the doctor's words but at least the flesh had healed some since the terrible accident.

"Of course not!" Isaac snapped with defensiveness. "I'm concerned about your health, not your appearance."

"Then let me go," Naomi replied firmly. "I need it."

Ultimately, Isaac agreed but Naomi could tell he did not like the idea.

"I'll go with you," he said as she gathered her small purse and draped a shawl over her homespun dress. The day was cooler than it had been all week and rain seemed to linger in the sky above.

"*Ach, Daed.* You and the others should work on the barn. The raising is this weekend, *yah*? You still have some clearing and work to do."

Isaac grimaced, knowing that his daughter was right.

"Please don't stay long," he begged, and Naomi nodded in agreement.

"I'll be a couple of hours," she conceded, heading out the front door.

She did not bother with the buggy. The rain was holding off and the walk would do her somewhat atrophied muscles good. Over the past week, Naomi had taken strolls about the property and tried to help the local men who were rushing to create a new barn in the wake of the fire, but Isaac had forbidden it.

As she walked, she thought about a potential reunion with Josiah. Whenever she had asked her father about him, Isaac had changed the subject or given a vague answer which told Naomi nothing.

He can't keep us apart forever, Naomi thought, quickening her step.

She found herself outside the market in a relatively short time, the morning shoppers already bustling about as she approached. Naomi suddenly wished she had asked Ruth for more details about where the Wengers shop was going to be, but she realized that it would not be that hard to find if she asked around.

And if I don't find the shop, I'll find out where he is, somehow.

As if God had heard her silent prayer, her eyes fell on the very man she had been seeking. Josiah's eyes locked with hers at the entranceway of the market, a startled expression on his face. At first, excitement colored his cheeks but as she drew nearer, his eyes darkened, and he looked away as though he was seeking an escape.

"Josiah!" she cried, joining his side. "I've missed you!"

She did not bother to keep her voice down, the joy of finally seeing him after so long overtaking all else.

"*Hallo*, Naomi," he muttered. "It's good to see you up and about."

There was a reservation to his words, as if he was addressing a customer rather than the woman he intended to marry. Purposefully, he turned his eyes away and stared at the ground.

"Has my *vadder* tried to call on you?" she asked, reaching for his hand. To Naomi's shock, he yanked his fingers back and stepped back to put distance between them. She stared at him imploringly.

"*Wat,* is it?" she asked. "What's wrong?"

"I think you should focus on your recovery," Josiah said, his eyes darting anywhere but on Naomi. "It's not a *gut* time for us to be together."

Shock and hurt flooded Naomi's heart as she gaped at him.

"I am recovered!" she protested, shaking her head in disbelief. Josiah finally raised his head and stared pointedly at her cheek, not bothering to hide his open disgust.

"No, you haven't," he replied shortly. "And you never will be."

Stunned, Naomi could not find her voice, even as Josiah turned away and disappeared back into the market without another word.

Did he shun me because of my disfigurement? Was his affection for me only skin deep?

Perhaps Naomi had suspected as much but the reality of Josiah openly and publicly shaming her in such a way stole her breath.

She knew she could not face the market now that he had rebuked her so severely and through a haze of tears, she rushed away.

Naomi could not see where she was going but when she finally stopped, she stood at a bridge in Ephrata Linear Park, staring blankly into the water below. Her mind was foggy, and she barely noticed the tears that had zigzagged down her cheeks as she dropped to her knees to pray.

Gott, why did you put Josiah in my path if only to take him away with this awful scar? Shame overcame her for doubting His plans, but Naomi could feel nothing but resentment. She had lost so much in such a short time.

She bowed her head and prayed that He would find a way to bring Josiah back to her. Naomi did not notice the presence of another until she heard the gentle clearing of a throat at her side. Her head whipped up and she gaped at Samuel Kropf.

"You!" she choked, trying to muster indignation at his arrival. "Have you come to mock me?"

Disbelief crossed over Samuel's face, overtaking the concern that had been imprinted previously.

"Mock you?" he echoed. "Why would I ever want to do that?"

More shame shot through Naomi, and she rose to her feet.

"Did you follow me from the market?" she asked.

"Yes... I saw you run off and I wanted to ensure you were all right," Sam conceded. A silence hung between them. "Are you alright?"

She met his eyes, noticing the way he held her gaze without flinching.

Doesn't he notice the scar on my face? Why isn't he giving me the same look of disgust that Josiah did?

"I'm fine," she tried to say haughtily but a fresh batch of tears made their way into her eyes as she spoke.

"Can I see you *deheem*?" Samuel asked softly. "I have a buggy."

She opened her mouth to refuse but it was not a refusal that escaped her lips.

"*Yah.*"

The answer was as much of a surprise to her as it was to Samuel who had clearly expected to be rejected again.

Rejected like Josiah rejected me.

The understanding hit Naomi like a slap but before she could speak, Samuel turned away.

"It's just up there," he told her. "I can bring it here if you don't want to see anyone."

His sympathy and compassion for her situation both endeared and angered Naomi.

"Why would I not want to see anyone?" she demanded hotly. "Because I'm too *mupsich?*"

Shock painted Samuel's face.

"You could never be ugly, Naomi," he said huskily. "A scar does not speak to one's heart."

Unexpectedly, Naomi felt heat rush through her body, and she locked eyes with Samuel again.

"*Es dutt mer*, Samuel," she apologized, realizing how unreasonable she was being to this kind man. "I'll come with you to the buggy."

They moved in silence, but Naomi caught Samuel sneaking glances at her face. At first, she was sure he was gawking at her injury but when she saw the glimmer of light in his eyes, she knew that was not the case at all.

"Why are you being so nice to me, Samuel?" she finally blurted out when they arrived at his cart. He helped her up before taking the reins and responding, as though he needed the time to weigh her question carefully.

"Why would I not be nice to you?" he finally countered. Naomi snorted, not caring about her manners.

"You know why," she muttered, turning her head away in embarrassment as he guided his horse away from town.

"We all have our problems, Naomi," Samuel replied quietly. "I would not like it if everyone held mine against me, especially in my time of need."

Naomi was about to argue that she was not in a time of need, but she thought better of her words. Samuel had just found her, sobbing. He did not need to be lied to.

"This injury has ruined my future," she moaned instead. "I will end up *en aldi Maed*."

To her surprise, Samuel chuckled.

"What's so funny?" she demanded, folding her arms over her chest.

"I can't imagine a world where Naomi Hershberger will ever be an old maid," he replied. Naomi frowned.

"That was before," she insisted. "You saw how Josiah treated me at the market."

"Josiah is a fool!" Samuel cried with far more passion than Naomi had ever heard him use. "You should be commended for your bravery. What did he do when the barn was burning?"

Naomi's lips parted but no sound escaped.

He tried to hold me back. He didn't try to help.

"It was dangerous," she mumbled, unsure of why she was still defending Josiah after how he had treated her but, in her mind, she realized that Samuel had a point.

"He didn't get burned," she added, shaking her head sadly. "He isn't disfigured. He did the right thing."

"If you hadn't gone in, your *vadder* would undoubtedly have died," Samuel replied shortly. A shudder passed through Naomi.

He's right about that too.

Suddenly, Naomi felt as though she was looking at Samuel Kropf with new eyes. Gone was the awkward, irritating boy she had always known and tried to avoid. In his place was a young man, fierce and loyal. Naomi swallowed the guilt rising in her throat.

Has he always been like this, and I've been too selfish to notice?

Samuel made a sound and Naomi looked where his eyes had rested.

"Have you not seen the damage from the fire?" she asked as she noted what he stared at.

"I have," Samuel confessed. "But it doesn't get any less shocking."

The buggy slowed before the Hershberger property and as it came to a stop, Samuel waited for Naomi to dismount. She paused and studied his face.

"Will you come back for *nachtesse?*" she asked impulsively. Samuel's eyes widened so much, they seemed ready to pop out of his head.

"H-here?" he sputtered in the manner that Naomi recalled so well. She swallowed her irritation with his stutter and nodded.

"*Yah*, of course," she said with a chuckle. Samuel nodded slowly and then more vehemently.

"*Yah*, I would like that," he agreed. "After work, I can come. Is seven o'clock, okay?"

"Seven is fine. The men are working late on the barn these days."

"I could help too if they're still going."

Appreciation shot through Naomi, and she moved to step off the buggy.

"Just come *esse*," she said. "You work hard enough during the day."

She stopped in front of the door to watch Samuel, but he seemed frozen in his spot. Abruptly, he lost the dazed look and grabbed for the reins again.

"See you tonight!" Naomi called. He waved as he disappeared, leaving Naomi to stand on the stoop.

She tried to process the new emotions that had settled inside her.

"Who was that?" Isaac asked, appearing from inside the house, his brow furrowed.

"Samuel Kropf. I've invited him for supper tonight."

Isaac did not respond but the sidelong look he cast his daughter said everything.

"He's a *freind, Daed*," she muttered, brushing past him to enter the house. Yet when she was alone, she found herself wondering when she had ever considered Samuel Kropf a friend before.

CHAPTER 7

Samuel spent his days working between two farms. One was owned by an Amish family by the name of Raber. The other was owned by a single, Englisch man with the surname Ashbrook. Of the two, Samuel preferred Ed Ashbrook who left the hands to themselves unless he had instructions or complaints.

The day he chanced upon Naomi in the market, Samuel had been out running errands for Ed and when he returned, he was floating on a cloud.

"You forgot the staples and tarp for the chicken coop," Ed informed him when he arrived back at the property. "I need those."

Embarrassed, Samuel offered to return to the market, but Ed waved him away.

"Never mind. I'll send Matthew, tomorrow."

He gave Samuel a look over his shoulder as if he could sense something was different about his farmhand, but he made no comment, to the younger man's relief.

Samuel's heart had not stopped beating wildly since dropping Naomi off at home.

This is the answer to my prayers, isn't it? Being invited to Naomi Hershberger's house for nachtesse?

He knew what his aunt would say about it.

"Why?" Amity asked suspiciously when he arrived home from work, rushing to wash and dress for the occasion. "What does she want from you?"

"*Nix!*" Samuel protested. "I think..."

He trailed off, worried about his aunt's ridicule.

"*Wat?* What do you think?"

"I think that the accident has changed her."

Amity snorted skeptically.

"People don't change, not for long, Sam. You are setting yourself up for disappointment."

"It's only supper, Amity," he grumbled, wishing he had not told her at all.

But the bit of shadow that his aunt had cast over him disappeared by the time he arrived at the Hershberger farm again that evening and his happiness was restored entirely when his eyes fell on Naomi.

He truly barely noticed the horrible scar on her face. Of course, he knew it was there but when he looked at Naomi, he only saw the girl he had always loved from afar.

"I'm glad you came, Sam," Naomi told him warmly, ushering him into the house. "*Nachtesse* is almost ready."

Isaac appeared in the front entranceway, a faint smile on his lips but his eyes raked over Samuel warily.

"*Hallo*, Samuel," Isaac said cordially. "How is your aunt?"

"She's well, *denki*." Samuel shifted his weight uncomfortably under Isaac's scrutiny, but Naomi broke up the awkwardness by leading them into the front room.

"Would you like something to drink?" Naomi offered. *"Wasser? Kaffe?"*

"Oh… no *kaffe* for me," Samuel mumbled, his cheeks reddening. "Water is *gut.*"

Naomi moved off to get his drink as the men settled into the front room. Samuel noted the bible sitting next to Isaac's chair.

"Did I interrupt your reading?" he asked nervously. His hands were clammy, and he wiped them on his pants.

"Nee," Isaac replied. "I read a passage or two after work every day to remind me of how blessed we are."

"Yah, I do the same," Samuel said, nodding. Isaac eyed him.

"Really?"

"Sometimes we forget our blessings," Samuel said, his pulse racing as he tried to get comfortable. "When strife hits."

"Indeed." Isaac stared at him thoughtfully as Naomi returned with his water and handed him the glass.

"*Komme* and sit at the table," she instructed. "*Nachtesse* is ready."

The men obliged, rising from their spots to follow Naomi into the dining room. Samuel smiled at the lovely food she had laid out. They sat and said their prayers before Naomi nodded for Samuel to eat.

"I'm relieved you were not hurt in the fire, Isaac," Samuel told him, taking a bite of his potatoes. Instantly, he realized that Naomi was not well-schooled in cooking. He managed to swallow the chunky, bland vegetable before putting his fork down.

"Thanks to my fearless daughter," Isaac agreed, looking lovingly at Naomi.

"She is very brave," Samuel conceded, also sneaking a glance at his hostess. She met his eyes and offered him a small smile before turning her eyes back to her plate.

"I did what anyone would have done," she insisted.

Not anyone. Not Josiah Wenger.

Samuel managed to keep his thoughts to himself.

"*Gott* protected our *familye* in His infinite wisdom," Isaac said, and Samuel nodded in agreement.

"Let's not talk about the fire," Naomi suggested, and the men looked at her contritely. "It has left me with enough memories to last a lifetime."

"Your scars will heal," Isaac said firmly but Samuel could hear the wavering conviction in his voice.

"It doesn't matter if they do," Samuel added. All eyes were on him now, but Samuel did not falter. "Beauty has nothing to do with the attractiveness of your face, Mimi."

Her smile was wider now, more genuine, and she blushed.

"He is a wise man, Mimi," Isaac said but he was looking at Samuel as though he was seeing him for the first time. "And he is right."

The remainder of their supper was filled with talk about work and the new barn. Samuel offered to help the men in the raising on the weekend and Isaac accepted, knowing that the event was a bonding experience in the community.

"I am exhausted," Isaac declared, barely finishing his meal. He laid his napkin on the table and rose as the younger generation stared in surprise. "I think I will retire for the *nacht*."

"Oh," Naomi said but it was all she did.

"*Guten nacht*," Samuel said as Isaac stepped away. "*Denki* for opening your home to me."

Isaac paused and offered him a look that Samuel did not understand.

"*Denki* for keeping your heart open, Sam," he replied, his voice barely audible. Naomi seemed startled by her father's words, but Isaac disappeared into the house, leaving the pair at the table.

"I'll help you with the dishes," Samuel offered when Naomi rose to clear off the plates. She looked at him in surprise.

"I can do it," she replied but Samuel took some plates anyway and returned them to the kitchen. When the task was finished and the dishes soaking, the duo retreated to the front of the house.

"I should get home," Samuel told her. "My aunt worries."

"I would worry too," Naomi told him with a coy kindness that Samuel had never heard before. He saw a different expression in her beautiful eyes now, one that he had prayed to see for as long as he could remember.

"Samuel…"

Her hand reached to touch him as he opened the door. Startled, Samuel almost jumped out of reach and Naomi smiled softly.

"I didn't mean to scare you."

"You didn't," he mumbled hastily but his cheeks flushed a deep red.

"Would you come back tomorrow, after work?"

Sam raised his head in confusion.

"Is there something you need?" he asked, distinctly aware of how her hand remained on his arm.

"*Yah,*" Naomi replied. "I would like for us to go on a walk and get to know one another."

The offer was just as stunning as the one for supper.

Nee, Samuel corrected himself. *This offer is more stunning. This is more. Naomi Hershberger is asking for more of me!*

His breaths were jagged and for a terrifying moment, he thought he might choke on the air that he simply breathed.

"If you don't want to, I'll understand," Naomi muttered, dropping her hand, disappointment overtaking her face. "I won't fault you."

"*Nee!*" Samuel almost yelled. Naomi's head jerked up.

"*Nee?*" she repeated in confusion. Samuel shook his head as if to get sense into it.

"I mean, *yah*," he corrected himself, forcing his mind to clear. "I would like that very much."

Relief crossed over her face, and she bobbed her head, her prayer bonnet slipping over her braid.

"Will you be finished at the same time tomorrow?" she asked. "Not that it matters. I am not going anywhere."

"I will be here a little earlier," Samuel promised, his tongue thick and awkward in his mouth. Naomi beamed.

"*Gut.* Until tomorrow then."

Samuel almost tripped over his own feet as he backed onto the porch and made his way toward his waiting wagon.

Amity was wrong! he thought with so much happiness, his heart almost exploded. *Maybe Naomi could love me after all.*

THE DAY'S end could not come fast enough for Samuel, and he knew that his work suffered in his excitement to see Naomi again, but he didn't care. He had never been so elated in his life and he intended to keep the feeling close.

Naomi waited on the porch for him when he arrived and instantly steered him toward the road.

"Is your *vadder* home?" Samuel asked, more to make conversation than curiosity.

"He is," Naomi replied. "But I didn't want him to see you."

Hurt shot through Samuel but before he could ask, Naomi continued, "He would start to talk your ear off, and our daylight hours would be wasted. I wanted this time just for us."

A smile crept onto Samuel's face.

"Oh."

She shot him a sidelong look.

"Do you ever see your *vadder*?" she asked quietly. Samuel returned her look, aghast.

"*Nee*, of course not!" he replied. "He's shunned."

"I know but…" she hesitated. "If that were my father, I don't know if I would be able to stay away."

"I was very young when he left the district," Samuel reminded her. "I wouldn't know him on the street if I were to walk past him."

Naomi cast him another strange look.

"*Wat*?" he asked, feeling slightly uncomfortable under her eyes. He felt as though she was trying to read into his soul.

"You seem so different than how we were as *kinner*."

"How's that?"

"You never had much to say when we were young and when you did, it was all stutters and mumbles."

Samuel flushed and Naomi instantly looked apologetic.

"I'm sorry," she said quickly. "I meant that… well, you seem more confident now."

He paused in his footsteps, the earliest recollections of his life slipping into his mind.

"Maybe that's because I learned long ago that if I spoke, my voice wouldn't be heard," he offered sadly. Shame touched Naomi's face.

"I didn't help matters, did I?" she breathed. "I have not treated you fairly."

"That is history now," Samuel said, picking up his pace again. Naomi hurried to catch up.

"I never had any trouble speaking my mind," she offered brightly after a moment of silence. "But I fear that will all change now."

"Why is that?" Samuel asked, perplexed. Naomi snorted and pointed to her face.

"You don't need to pretend with me, Sam."

Samuel sighed and again stopped walking, turning to face her fully.

"I don't see your scars," he told her earnestly. "I see your inner beauty. Moreover, you can always say whatever it is you have on your mind to me."

A look of tenderness fell over Naomi's face, and she gave Sam the warmest smile yet.

"*Denki*, Sam," she breathed, locking eyes with him. "I will never forget the kindness you've shown me."

And Samuel truly believed her.

CHAPTER 8

*N*aomi could not deny that she enjoyed her walks with Samuel. Every night after work, he would hurry to her house, sometimes in his work clothing. He knew all the hidden places in Ephrata, little nooks and the forest that Naomi, in all her life, had never heard of.

"When you spend enough time alone, you learn all the hideaways," Samuel explained without any bitterness.

He showed her his favorite cave in the nearby ravines and some nights, he took her for supper in town.

On Sam's arm, Naomi almost forgot about her burns. If not for the odd stare and whisper, she might have entirely forsaken her scars.

One night, Isaac asked her the question she had been wondering for herself.

"Will you marry Sam Kropf?"

Even though she had been thinking it in her own mind, hearing the words aloud gave Naomi a shiver of apprehension. Two months ago, she would have laughed in the face of anyone making such a suggestion, but these days, Sam had become such an important part of her life.

Important enough to spend the rest of my life with?

It was something she knew she would have to pray upon.

She did not answer her father and instead retreated to her bedroom to do exactly that. She knelt next to her bed and contemplated.

Gott, I think Samuel will ask me to marry him. What will I do? Is he the one I'm meant to be with?

As she slipped into her bed that night and closed her eyes, the image of Sam's bright eyes and blond curls painted before her eyelids.

Naomi took it as a good sign before she fell into a dreamless sleep.

HER HAND CURLED around the wicker basket as Naomi made her way onto the yard the next morning to collect the eggs.

"Guten mariye."

She stopped dead in her tracks at the sound of a familiar voice, the blood draining from her face. Whirling about, she stared into Josiah's charming smile. Instantly, her hand moved to her cheek to hide the burns, but today, Josiah did not seem to notice.

"W-wat are you doing here?" she choked, a whirlwind of emotions flooding her. The sight of him brought back all the feelings she thought she had repressed, his misdeeds forgotten in that instant.

"Let me take that," Josiah suggested, reaching for the basket. She did not argue as he took it from her hands, her mouth still parted. He marched toward the chicken coop and Naomi had no choice but to follow after him.

"Josiah, why are you here?" she demanded again as they entered the coop.

Sighing, he turned to her.

"I have come to apologize," he confessed. "I've been a fool, a *sau*."

He paused, his eyes trailing over her face before quickly looking away.

"I was in shock after your accident," he went on. "And I handled it all so badly."

The words were bittersweet. Naomi had hoped to hear them but that had been weeks ago, before she had developed feelings for Samuel.

"What are you saying?" she asked, her voice squeaking slightly. Josiah gave her one of his boyish smiles.

"I'm saying that we can still be married."

The sentence hit Naomi with a thud, and she gaped at him disbelievingly.

"You want to get married, now?" she asked, unable to keep the contempt from her words. "I haven't seen you in weeks!"

She did not remind him that the last time she had seen him, he had been unnecessarily cruel.

"I know," Josiah conceded, sighing again. "But I had to take time to deal with your…"

He waved his hand toward her face.

"I'm over that now," he continued quickly. "And we should announce our betrothal."

Confusion overwhelmed Naomi.

I prayed to Gott last night and this is what He sends me as an answer?

She would be lying to say that she did not have strong feelings for Josiah but after all that had happened, could she ever really trust him again?

"Why do you look so uncertain?" Josiah demanded, his vivid eyes darkening. "Isn't that what you wanted?"

"I…" Naomi faltered but before she could collect her thoughts, the coop door opened. To her utter horror, Samuel stood at the threshold, his smile fading away as he took in the scene before him.

"What is he doing here?" Samuel cried, an accusing look on his face. Josiah snorted loudly.

"What am I doing here?" he repeated. "I'm visiting my betrothed. Who are you?"

Samuel's face twisted into a look of anguish that pierced Naomi's soul.

"You would marry him after all he's done to you?" Samuel demanded, his voice cracking slightly. "All he cares about is your beauty."

"Well, that's not really true now if I'm willing to marry her anyway," Josiah shot back but Naomi saw the way he eyed her burns. "Anyway, she doesn't need to answer to you. Off you go."

"I'm not going anywhere!" Samuel yelled defensively. Naomi felt a combination of sadness and anger, although she wasn't sure for whom the feelings were for.

"You're not needed here." Josiah frowned, advancing on Samuel, even though the blond man was taller by several inches. "You interrupted a private conversation."

Again, Samuel turned toward Naomi, but she could not find her voice. Whatever he saw in her face seemed to answer his unspoken question. Without a word, he spun and tripped over himself, almost landing on his face. Josiah whooped with amusement as Samuel half-crawled out the door.

Naomi stared at Josiah in shock, her ire growing.

"You're lucky I came along," he said with a chuckle. "Otherwise, you'd be married to the likes of him. Can you imagine?"

Naomi's eyes narrowed to slits.

"Why have you had a change of heart?" she asked bluntly. "You can barely look at me, even now, and you claim to want to marry me?"

Josiah's smile faltered.

"I told you," he mumbled, scuffing his shoe into the sawdust. "I realized that I still love you."

"*Nee,* that's not true."

The door had opened again and neither had noticed Isaac until he spoke. The anger in her father was almost palpable as he glowered at Josiah.

"Of course, it is," Josiah replied loudly, his face paling.

Naomi bristled, she was beginning to see Josiah for who he really was, realizing how close she had come to making a terrible mistake.

Isaac stepped forward. "Your parents have caught you fornicating with an *Englisch* girl. You're only trying to marry my daughter to cover your tracks and continue your *verboden* affair," Isaac said dully.

Josiah gaped as Naomi gasped, her stomach roiling.

"Th-that's not true!" Josiah tried to choke out but Isaac shook his head.

"More people know about it than you realize. It's all over town. Your secret is out, and Bishop Troyer is looking for you. Leave before you cast more shame on my *familye*, Josiah."

To his credit, Josiah did not argue and instead rushed from the coop, almost tripping in precisely the same place that Samuel had moments before.

Tears welled up in Naomi's eyes and Isaac closed the short distance between them.

"Are you alright?" he demanded. "Did he harm you?"

Naomi shook her head and sniffled.

"*Nee*, not physically, anyway," she breathed, brushing past her father. "But I have hurt Samuel. Again."

CHAPTER 9

*I*ntuitively, Naomi headed toward the ravines. She could still hear Samuel's words in her head about where he would go when he was feeling unwanted. She was sure that he would not want to be around others after what had happened.

Every step she took, the sky above her head grew darker, as though God was unhappy for the way she had behaved.

Why did I not try to stop him? Why didn't I tell him to stay?

Naomi replayed the terrible scene over and over in her head as rain began to fall around her. Even the thickness of the trees, could not protect her skin from the driving rain and soon, she found herself at the cave.

Yet as she entered, her heart grew heavier. There was no sign of Samuel there. If he had been there, he had since moved on.

Helplessly, she stood at the mouth of the cave, silently willing Samuel to come to her. Mud stuck to her bare feet as she set off through the brambles toward the road. Above her, thunder rumbled deeply. Naomi thought about what she was going to say when she saw Samuel, about how she was going to win him back after the way she had acted.

If he doesn't forgive me, I'll have no one but myself to blame.

Her feet splashed through the puddles and more water pelted from the sky to soak through her dress. She shivered slightly but not from cold.

Up head, she saw Amity's tiny house and she ran the rest of the way to pound on the door.

In seconds, Amity opened the door to the girl. A look of disapproval painted her face the moment she laid eyes on Naomi.

"Have you no sense at all, running around in the rain?" she asked chidingly.

"Is Samuel here?" Naomi demanded, ignoring Amity's judging look. She gazed behind the older woman for any indication that he was present, but she saw nothing. The expression of concern on Amity's face only fueled Naomi's worry.

"*Nee*... said he was coming to you this *mariye*. Did you not see him?"

Rain continued to pour from the sky, a clap of thunder echoing through the fields and Naomi jumped.

"I did but..." Naomi could not bring herself to explain what had happened. She was sure that Amity did not approve of her relationship with Samuel, and this would only solidify what the older woman suspected.

"I have to find him," Naomi mumbled, spinning away.

"Foolish girl, *komme* inside and wait!" Amity yelled after her. "He'll be back sooner or later."

Naomi paused and glanced over her shoulder, shaking her matted hair.

"*Nee*, I can't wait," she replied, tears welling in her eyes. She was grateful for the unexpected storm. It would keep Amity from seeing her tears.

"You'll catch your death tromping around in the rain!" Amity called but Naomi ignored her. She did not care about getting wet or sick. She only cared about Samuel.

Half-running, her feet slipping in the mud as she moved, Naomi wracked her brain for all the other places that Samuel had taken her over the past few weeks.

I'll start with the closest and work my way outward, she thought when her feet touched the road again but as she looked up, she saw him.

His head was down, weighted by the rain and his own sorrow, shoulders hunched. To Naomi, he looked as though he might topple over with every step.

Without hesitation, she raced toward him, her heart hammering wildly in her chest.

"Sam!" she cried. His head lifted but the process seemed laborious. He stared at her with dead, unhappy eyes. The mere sight of his face stopped her a few feet from where he stood.

"Sam, I'm sorry!" she breathed, extending a hand toward him. "I made a terrible mistake."

"You shouldn't be here," he said flatly. "Josiah will be angry."

"Josiah was using me as a way to placate his *leit*," Naomi said. Samuel's face twisted even deeper into unhappiness, and she immediately realized what he was thinking. "Not that it matters!"

"Mimi, I care about you," Samuel told her, his voice almost carrying into the wind. "I want you to be happy, even if it isn't with me."

"I know now that I can only be happy with you, Sam," she insisted, closing the short gap between them. "I have been such a fool, falling for a man like Josiah when you have been here all along. I was blinded by what I saw on the outside, but I know now that none of that matters. Only a man with a good heart will make me happy. You are that man, Sam."

A glimmer of hope shone in Samuel's eyes, but he did not relent.

"I don't know what to believe," he replied honestly. "You didn't say a word when Josiah claimed you as his own."

Naomi hung her head in shame.

"I have made many mistakes in my life. I see that now. I was like Josiah in so many ways, which was I was drawn to him. But I am changing, Sam, because of you. You have shown me that there is so much more to life than who is the most established or the most handsome... not that you are not handsome."

Samuel did not respond but his eyes spoke to her, and she was encouraged to go on.

"I have put you through so much, even when we were children. I don't blame you if you won't accept this. I have a lot of work to do on myself but whatever you decide, I want you to know that my feelings for you are genuine."

This time, Sam did not try to hide the shimmer in his eyes. He reached for her hands and drew her close before she realized what was happening.

"Do you know how long I've prayed to hear those words from your mouth?" he asked, his voice raspy.

"Every night, I have asked *Gott* to protect you and keep you safe."

"Your prayers have worked," she told him sincerely. "As have mine."

"You prayed for me?" Samuel asked dubiously.

"*Yah*," she replied honestly. "I prayed for *Gott* to send me a perfect husband, and He sent you to me."

Samuel chuckled, his hands cupping her face softly to stare into her eyes.

"I am far from perfect," he replied humbly. "But I will care for you better than anyone ever could. That is my promise to you."

"You are perfect for me," Naomi breathed, feeling the burn of tears behind her eyes. "Even if I am flawed."

"You are perfect to me in every way," Samuel countered, drawing her face closer, his large hands covering her scars. Their lips met and tingles of hope flooded through Naomi's body.

This is what I have waited for my entire life, she thought with growing joy. *I sought the wrong things for so long and now, I finally have what's right.*

A spark of lightning cracked through the sky and forced them apart.

"We should get inside before we drown." Samuel laughed, tugging on her hand.

"One more minute," Naomi begged, pulling him back into her arms. She wanted to relish the moment that she had found and accepted Samuel into her life.

Gott always knows, she thought gratefully, burying her face into Samuel's muscled chest. *All we need is faith.*

EPILOGUE

THREE MONTHS LATER...

*T*he buggy slid over the freshly fallen snow, but the horse carried herself with aplomb and navigated the conditions without issue.

"You could have waited until spring to be married," Amity complained, but for once, Samuel heard a lilt of pride in her voice.

"Why wait any longer?" he replied, shrugging his shoulders. "We have already waited a lifetime."

Amity huffed but through his peripheral vision, Samuel caught the appreciative look on her face.

She has warmed to the idea of me marrying Naomi, he thought happily. He had not realized how much stock he put into his aunt's approval until recently.

As if reading his thoughts, Amity spoke softly.

"I was wrong about Naomi," she mumbled.

"*Komme* again?" Samuel choked. He was not sure he had heard properly but when he met Amity's eyes, he realized that he had heard just fine.

"I wasn't always wrong about her," Amity insisted, folding her arms over her thick cloak. "But since her accident, she has changed, humbled. I don't worry about her for you anymore."

Relief sank into Samuel's bones, and he offered his aunt a warm smile.

"I'm glad to hear it, Amity."

"I hope you know, Sam, that anything I have ever told you has been to save you from the pain I have endured."

"As all good parents do for their *kinner*," Samuel replied gently. Amity's face glowed with appreciation.

"I'm not your parent," she said.

"You are the only parent I have ever had," Samuel told her earnestly. "And I'm glad I had you."

He stopped the cart in front of the Hershberger's house and escorted his aunt to the front. Guests had already begun to arrive, the district women bringing cakes and pies to celebrate. Bishop Troyer waited impatiently for him near the front room.

"You're late," he chided Samuel.

"*Nee*, I'm not," Samuel argued. Bishop Troyer gaped at him, stunned at his bold response but when he glanced at the grandfather clock in the corner, he flushed with embarrassment.

"*Yah*, you're right." He chuckled. "I was early."

"Where is the bride-to-be?" Samuel asked, looking around.

"I'm here, Samuel."

His breath was stolen at the sight of her beauty. She wore a light blue gown with long sleeves and lace trim, her long hair twisted into a garland braid around her head.

Someone had found her a veil for her to wear and Naomi peered out from behind it with timid eyes.

"Where did you get that?" Samuel asked, troubled by the sight of it.

"An *Englisch* girl in town gave it to me. She said it would hide my scars."

Slowly, careful not to muss her hair, Samuel removed it from her crown.

"Wait! What are you doing?" Naomi protested.

"This isn't tradition," he said quietly, tossing the veil onto the floor.

"*Nee*, but Samuel, my face—"

"Is the most beautiful face in the district. It always has been and will continue to be until our daughter takes that title. It is the face that I am marrying, not a piece of mesh cloth to hide you eyes and soul behind."

"Samuel, that's very sweet but the guests…"

"I want the guests to see the woman I am marrying, Naomi. You don't need to hide yourself. You have nothing to be ashamed of."

Naomi pressed her lips together and Samuel worried that he might have overstepped his bounds with her but when she looked up, he realized that her eyes were glistening with unshed tears.

"Mimi, I want you to be happy," he murmured, stepping closer to her. "If the veil is that important to you…"

"*Nee*," she sniffled, shaking her head as she hastily wiped away her tears. "It's not. All that is important to me is here, in this room."

She nodded toward her father, sitting in a corner among a group of other men but his eyes were fixed on the pair, his smile wide and genuine.

"You and my *vadder* are all that I care about. If you can accept me as I am then I won't ever try to hide myself again."

"I have always loved you for who you are," Samuel told her earnestly. "And I always will."

"Are we ready to start the ceremony?" Bishop Troyer said, frowning slightly from behind them.

Samuel and Naomi nodded and followed Bishop Troyer out the back door toward the barn as the women gathered the guests to follow.

As they moved, a light rain began to fall from the sky, the droplets falling like tears on the pair.

Both Naomi and Samuel looked upward in disbelief.

"Why does it always rain at these moments?" Naomi asked, echoing Samuel's very thoughts. He paused, cupping her face in his hands, smiling softly.

"Because *Gott* weeps for us," he replied. Naomi seemed shocked by the answer.

"Weeps for us?" she echoed.

"*Yah*," Samuel said softly, kissing her forehead. "He weeps tears of joy for us and our future together..."

~*~*~

I do hope that you enjoyed reading '*Love's Perfect Imperfection*.'

May I suggest that you might also like to read my '*Amish Christmas Blessings*' 15 Book Box Set that readers are loving!

Available on Amazon for just $0.99 or Free with Kindle Unlimited simply by clicking on the link below.

Click here to get your copy of 'Amish Christmas Blessings - 15 Book Box Set' - Today!

Sample of Chapter One

Although the snow had yet to fall on Holmes County, Rose Lapp could smell the scent of Christmas in the air. It was a subtle difference from the previous week but one that Rose knew well—almost inherently. The last of the Thanksgiving décor, boasting the time of Englisch gratitude, had been packed away the previous weekend and Killbuck was alive with new lights and green wreaths upon the posts and poles. It was the same scene that played out every year at this time, yet it never ceased to excite Rose, just as it did her peers. In the coming weeks, garlands and nativity sets would appear, together with boisterous Santa Clauses to appease the English children, and snatches of Christmas carols would be heard in the English booths. Every year, the holiday season crept into town, slowly and by osmosis, until everyone was fully enthralled in the spirit of the season, almost without noticing.

The market was busier than it had been in the previous weeks, yet another indicator that the holiday was near. A charged excitement always seemed to flow through the stalls, infectiously from one person to the next, regardless of whether they were English or Amish. Even at this point of the season, tourists made their rounds into Amish country, wanting to fill their stockings and load their trees with handmade items that could only be found in the area. They worked in tandem all the year, the two cultures, but there was an even closer bond between them now, despite their faith-based differences. Christmas did nothing if not bring people together and Rose loved everything about it.

She smiled and nodded at several of her friends and neighbors, painfully aware of the fact that she towered over most of them. At six feet in height, she had always seemed to overshadow anyone who crossed her path, even in bare feet. It did not matter that Rose had a lovely face with bright blue eyes or long, silk-spun hair which caught glints of gold, even in the late autumn sun. No one could look past her unusual stature, especially not men who were much more interested in the daintier qualities of her female peers. At twenty-four, Rose was certain that she was bound to be unmarried, a fact that she was slowly coming to terms with, even if it were difficult, not only on her but her mother too. She saw several happy couples and their offspring every day, none more so than in town and it sent pangs of melancholy through Rose's heart. She tried to hold faith, as her mother always suggested, but it was becoming increasingly difficult as the years passed. All the eligible men in her community seemed to be married and while Rose was not an old woman, she was beginning to feel like one. So many of her acquaintances had two or even three children by now.

Gott has other plans for me, she told herself firmly, turning away from yet another giggling child who clung to the hem of her mother's dress. *And I am blessed to have gut familye. So many others do not have what I do.*

She knew she was merely echoing her mother's own words, but she wondered if Evelyn truly did feel that way or if her mother resented not being a grandmother. Rose was her only child, after all. If she did not bear children, no one would be left to call her "*Grossmammi.*"

She had not realized she had paused in front of a booth until she heard her name called.

"*Guten mariye*, Rose," Leah Yoder said, beaming at her new customer, bringing Rose back to the present reality.

"*Guten mariye*," Rose replied in her usual, pleasant way.

"I have blackcurrant jam today. It's your *mudder's* favorite, isn't it?" Leah replied, eager to make the sale as she always was. Rose nodded. She shoved away any of the negative thoughts that had threatened to creep into her mind and focussed on the jars in front of her. There were dozens of flavors to choose from and while she was not in need of jam, she did not want to leave Leah's booth empty handed. She had inadvertently stopped, and it felt bad to look without purchasing something.

"I'll take two jars of the blackcurrant" she concluded, eying the strawberry as Leah stared pointedly at her, waiting for her to order more. Swallowing a sigh, Rose nodded at another random container. "And one of these too."

Maybe Mamm would like to make some pies this week for karrich, she mused, knowing that Evelyn would have something to say about her impulsive purchases. There was no plan to make pies for worship and bringing home excess would surely annoy Evelyn. But it was too late now.

"*Yah?* Are you sure you don't want some peach or blueberry?" Leah asked coyly, sensing that she might be able to make a better sale if she pushed just slightly. Rose's good nature was easy to exploit but the young woman reminded herself that there was a budget to be maintained. With her father gone now, pennies had to be watched and jam was a luxury they could do without. But that had not stopped Rose from accepting Leah's forced sale.

"The three jars are plenty," Rose said firmly even though it made her feel slightly guilty. She avoided Leah's eyes as she fumbled for her purse from inside one of the cloth bags she carried.

Don't be foolish, she warned herself, shooing away the shame. *If I overbought everywhere, Mamm and I would lose our haus.*

Even knowing this, she could not stifle the sense that she could do more.

Leah shrugged and offered her a total for the purchases.

"There you are, Rose. *Komme* back soon!" Leah said brightly, handing her the jars and Rose turned, her attention on placing the breakable items carefully in her bag. There was little to cushion the glass inside and she frowned as she concentrated on the task as she spun around without looking. She did not realize there was a man behind her until she collided with him, almost dropping one of the blackcurrant containers. With shockingly quick reflexes, the man caught the jar with his left hand and righted his body, holding the container, a broad smile overtaking his face. To Rose's additional surprise, he was taller than she was, with gentle brown eyes and a crop of dark-blond hair. She found herself looking up at him, a combination of gratitude and humiliation overcoming her. For a moment, she did not know what to say. Finally, she found her voice.

"Goodness," she breathed apologetically. "*Es dutt mer leed!*"

The young man's grin widened, and he handed the jar back to her, shaking his head. He seemed to be a few years younger than Rose, perhaps twenty or twenty-one. But that did not seem relevant in the moment, her breath partially stolen by his face. She could not pull her gaze away and when she realized she was gawking, a deep flush tinged her cheeks.

"No harm done," he assured her, his voice kind and soft. "I'm glad it didn't break."

His eyes brightened as they took in her expression and Rose tried to place him. He was certainly Amish, she saw, his accent the same as hers and his clothes homespun. The customary white shirt and suspenders were a giveaway but beyond that, he was unfamiliar to her. She was sure she would have recalled such an attractive man in the district, having lived there her whole life but the harder she stared at him, the less she could figure out who he might be. No, this was a stranger—albeit one who was beaming at her with interest.

If he belonged here, he wouldn't be smiling at me like that, Rose thought, gulping back her nervousness.

Without pausing to consider her next words, she blurted out, "Are you new here? In town, I mean?"

Despite her immediate embarrassment, his grin broadened again, and he nodded eagerly. He seemed relieved to have someone to speak with and Rose was eager to take in all she could about him.

"*Yah,*" he conceded. "I only just arrived in Holmes County. I'm learning my way around and my *grossdaddi* suggested I come to the market. So far, he has given me good advice."

"Oh…" Rose looked down at her hands, feeling the blush grow to snake down her pale neck. She was grateful for the heavy coat she wore, certain that her face was crimson and, under the garish lights of the market, impossible to overlook.

"I'm sorry I almost knocked you off your feet," she mumbled, unsure of what else to say. She did not want to be presumptuous about his friendly chatter, but she could not deny that she felt an immediate attraction to this man.

"Sometimes, those are the most worthwhile encounters," he replied easily. "My name is Gabriel Fisher."

Rose's head jerked back up and she met his eyes.

Fisher. I know who he is!

Excitement shot through her as she realized that this man might not be as much of a stranger as she had initially thought.

"Are you related to Abram?" she asked, her pulse quickening. The newly widowed man lived only a few farms away from where Rose stayed with her mother, and she knew him well enough.

"*Yah*, he's my *grossdaddi*. I came here from Pennsylvania to care for him after my *grossmammi* died."

Rose's heart quickened more, and she felt a rush of admiration for the young man.

"I am sorry for your loss," she said softly. "Your *grossmammi* was a *gut frau*."

She meant her words, recalling Grace Fisher's gentle demeanor and kindness.

"I never really got a chance to know her too well," Gabriel confessed, sounding shamed. "My *vadder* is from here but when he moved to Pennsylvania to be with my *mudder*, he did not come back often. I think there was some kind of *familye* disagreement about it."

If there had been, Rose did not know much about it.

"Anyway, now that *Grossdaddi* has no one, my *vadder* thought I should come back here... so here I am."

"That is very kind of you," Rose said sincerely. She could not imagine having to uproot her entire existence to live with family she did not know. "My *mudder* and I know your *grossdaddi* well. He's a *gut* man too."

Gabriel's smile remained and he nodded but Rose thought she saw a shadow cross over his face.

"It's *gut* to spend time with him," he agreed. "You never did tell me your name."

"Oh!" Rose chuckled nervously. "Rose. Rose Lapp."

"It's nice to meet you, Rose Lapp." They nodded at one another, a small silence falling between them again before Rose filled it with uneasy chatter. She was not sure what to make of the way Gabriel was staring at her, but she could feel her insides twisting under his stare.

"Maybe we could see about having you over for *nachtesse* one night," Rose went on with uncharacteristic boldness. She was not accustomed to being so forward but there was something disarming about Gabriel Fisher, something that told her that she could be herself. His face brightened more, and she was doubly relieved that she had spoken her mind.

"*Yah*, that would be *gut!*" he said, sounding relieved. "I don't know many people here and my *grossdaddi* doesn't seem to have people around much. I guess he preferred his privacy."

"I'm sure that will change soon. The community is friendly, and you will meet lots of people."

A young man as attractive as Gabriel would have no trouble making acquaintances and eventually finding a courtship if that was what he was seeking. Yet, in that moment, his eyes fixed only on her as if he were oblivious to the dozens of people who walked by, Rose permitted herself to hope. He did not seem to notice the curious looks of the Amish passersby who not only failed to recognize him but wondered who was wasting their time speaking with the awkward Rose Lapp.

"I'll speak to my *mudder*," Rose promised, more color tinging her already flushed cheeks. "About *nachtesse* this week. Maybe Tuesday or Thursday?"

"I look forward to it," Gabriel told her, and she could hear the sincerity in his voice. "I think it will be good for my *grossdaddi* too. He shouldn't spend so much time alone. It's making him even sadder."

He looked around guiltily, but Rose smiled.

"He was by himself with your *grossmammi* for a long time. It will take some getting used to."

"It will help if I have help," Gabriel said confidently, and Rose smiled happily. Swallowing her nervousness, Rose finally packed the jam properly in her cloth bag and adjusted the strap on her shoulder.

"I should be getting *deheem*," she murmured, wishing she could think of an excuse to stay. "My *mudder* is expecting me, and I'm already late."

"We'll see each other soon," Gabriel said with assuredness that made Rose like him even more. They bid one another goodbye, and Rose hurried off, distinctly aware that he was watching her go. She paused at the end of the row and hesitatingly looked back. To her amazement, Gabriel still stared after her, a wide grin on his face. Their eyes locked for a moment before she reluctantly hurried away. Rose almost skipped into the parking lot to find her buggy, her own smile spreading from one ear to the next. She could not wait to tell her mother about the new friend she had made in town.

She'll be so happy to hear that he's taller than me!

Click here to get your copy of 'Amish Christmas Blessings - 15 Book Box Set' - Today!

A NOTE FROM THE AUTHOR

Dear Reader,

I do hope that you enjoyed reading '**Love's Perfect Imperfection**'

Possibly you even identify with the characters in some small way. Many of us presume to know God's will for our lives, and don't realize that His timing often does not match our own.

The foremost reason that I love writing about the Amish is that their lifestyle is diametrically opposed to the Western norm. The simplicity and purity evident there is so vastly refreshing that the story lines derived from them are suitable for everyone.

Be sure to keep an eye out for the next book which is coming soon.

Emma Cartwright

Thank You!

Thank you for purchasing this book. We hope that you have enjoyed reading it.

If you enjoyed reading this book **please may you consider leaving a review** — it really would help greatly to get the word out!

Newsletter

If you love reading sweet, clean, Amish Romance stories why not join Emma Cartwright's newsletter and receive advance notification of new releases and more!

Simply sign up here: http://eepurl.com/dgw2I5

And get your *FREE* copy of **Amish Unexpected Love**

Contact Me

If you'd simply like to drop us a line you can contact us at **emma@emmacartwrightbooks.com**

You can also connect with me on my new **Facebook page.**

I will always let you know about new releases on my Facebook page, so it is worth liking that if you get the chance.

LIKE EMMA'S FB PAGE HERE

I welcome your thoughts and would love to hear from you!

I will then also be able to let you know about new books coming out along with Amazon special deals etc

Made in the USA
Monee, IL
02 April 2022

94007540R10075